SCHOLASTIC READER
LEVEL 2
250-750 WORDS

School Day!

By Jenne Simon
Illustrated by Prescott Hill

SCHOLASTIC INC.

New York   Toronto   London   Auckland

Sydney   Mexico City   New Delhi   Hong Kong

ISBN 978-0-545-40321-4

12 11 10 9 8 7 6 5   13 14 15 16 17/0

Designed by Angela Jun
Printed in the U.S.A.   40
First printing, July 2012

Bea Spells-a-Lot had just finished a good book.
She had learned some new things.
But she wanted to learn even more.
Then Bea had a great idea!

Bea invited many of her friends over for School Day.

Each person would teach the group a lesson.

That way everyone would learn lots of new things!

"What will you teach us?" Bea asked
Misty Mysterious.

Misty smiled. "It's a secret," she said.

Bea could not wait to find out what
it was!

Blossom Flowerpot went first. She showed the group how to grow a plant.

"First you make a hole," said Blossom. "Then you plant a seed. Then you water it. And then you wait for it to grow."

"I don't like waiting!" cried Bea.

"I know it can be hard," Blossom laughed. "But with lots of water and sunlight—and a little bit of love—we'll have a pretty flower in no time!"

Marina Anchors taught the group about the ocean.

"The water in the ocean is salty," said Marina.

"What kinds of animals live there?" asked Bea.

"Whales and dolphins and lots of fish!" said Marina.

"Have you ever been in the ocean?" asked Misty.

"No," said Marina. "I would love to. But first I need to learn how to swim!"

Spot Splatter Splash gave a painting lesson. "There are seven colors in the rainbow," she said. "And they are all beautiful!"

Spot handed out paper and brushes. Then everyone began to paint.

"I made a mistake!" cried Bea.

"It doesn't matter" Spot said, "as long as you're having fun!"

Pillow Featherbed taught everyone
ways to help themselves fall asleep.
"You can drink warm milk, read a bedtime
story, or count sheep."

"One, two, three . . ." said Pillow.
Pillow curled up as she counted.
Soon she was asleep!

Next Dot Starlight talked about the stars and planets.

"It takes a whole year for Earth to go all the way around the sun," she said.

"What do you think it's like in space?" Bea asked.

Dot thought for a moment. "I'm not sure. But when I grow up, I'm going to try to find out!"

Berry Jars 'N' Jam and Sunny Side Up love animals.

So they taught everyone how to care for their pets.

"Give them food and water every day," Sunny said.

"And a bath when they are dirty," Berry added.

Berry rubbed her cow behind the ears. "Some animals like to be petted," she said. "And some like to talk," Sunny said to her chick.

CHEEP! CHEEP!

Everyone practiced caring for their own pets.
But Bea was distracted. She could not stop
thinking about Misty's secret.

"Won't you give me just one little hint?" she begged Misty.

Misty shook her head. "That would ruin the surprise!"

Patch Treasurechest loved to collect things.
He showed everyone how to keep a collection.

Crystals

Large Shells

Button

Sea Glass

Small Shells

Pearls

"I label each treasure," said Patch. "That way I will never forget where and when I found it."

"What a great way to hold on to special memories!" said Bea.

Peanut Big Top's lesson was full of ups and downs. She showed everyone how to cartwheel.

At first, she went up, up, up. And then she came crashing down, down, down!

Uh-oh!

Luckily, Rosy Bumps 'N' Bruises was there to
show them how to bandage a scraped knee.
Rosy really likes bandages!

Then it was cookie time! Crumbs Sugar Cookie's lesson was about baking.

"This recipe has five parts: flour, eggs, butter, sugar, and good friends to help out!" said Crumbs.

She showed them how to mix the batter, roll the dough, and shape the cookies.

"Now we just have to bake the cookies and wait," said Crumbs.

"Oh, no! More waiting?" cried Bea.

"I know these cookies will be worth waiting for!" Crumbs said.

Then Misty tapped Bea on the arm.
"It's finally time for my lesson," Misty said.
"I'm going to teach you a magic trick!"
"What a great surprise!" said Bea.

Misty showed everyone her magic top hat.
"Look. There's nothing inside," she said.
Everyone could see that was true.

Then Misty reached inside the hat . . . and pulled out her pet rabbit!

"Wow!" everyone shouted.

The School Day was almost over.
But before it was time to go, Bea heard
something that was sure to make everyone smile.
DING! The cookies were ready.

Bea handed Misty a cookie and a glass of milk. "I'm glad you kept your lesson a secret," said Bea. "Surprises can be fun!"

Bea took a bite of her cookie.

The day had been filled with lots of sweet surprises.

"We may be different," she said. "But we all have something special to share."